I0692282

Seven Stories for Christmas

LONGCROSS PRESS

Published by Longcross Press

P.O. Box 161, Battle, TN33 3DG, England

vonb@pt.lu

ISBN 9780956098344

Seven Stories for Christmas

by

Henry von Blumenthal

LONGCROSS PRESS

LONGCROSS PRESS

Seven Stories for Christmas

Henry von Blumenthal was born in 1961. He was educated at Westminster School and Christ Church, Oxford, where he read Theology. He lives in Luxembourg, where he works for the European Investment Bank, currently as the Spokesman for the staff representation.

Also published by Longcross Press is *The Companion to British History* by his late father Charles Arnold-Baker (born Wolfgang von Blumenthal), of which he is the editor.

To Nieves

with love

CONTENTS

PREFACE

My late father, Charles Arnold-Baker, used to send out Christmas cards with a story. In 2005 he announced that, at 87, he was too old to carry on with this, so I decided that year to continue the custom myself.

My father's stories were invariably humorous and conveyed all that is best of the Christmas spirit; and they were always learned, as was he.

The stories in this little book were not really written with a particular readership in mind. Each year, about Eastertide, they seem to have suggested themselves, I am unable to say exactly how, except that they are the product of research, meditation and above all gratitude to St. Luke. To his inspiration and, I dare say, intercession, I owe a great deal, not least part of a revolution in my life which made me, I hope, a more bearable husband than I might otherwise have been; hence the dedication of this book to my wife of three patient decades.

Every year I get a number of requests for explanations of the background to the subject matter of these stories, so I have appended notes which the reader may find interesting to consult in conjunction with a Bible. I have mostly used the Catholic Douay-Rheims translation by Bishop Challoner of 1752.

HvB
Lameschmillen, Luxembourg,
October 18 2013

**St Luke Painting a Portrait
of the Virgin Mary by Guercino, 1652**

1. MARY

"I did not send for a doctor. Thank God, I am in the best of health."

She certainly was. Although it was possible to see that she must be in her seventies, she was remarkably fine-looking, beautiful even, for her age. Standing at the large front door of her house, she held it open with a welcoming smile, her face, slightly wrinkled from past cares and present smiles, framed by the head-covering of her robe of blackest blue.

"You are right, madam, I am a doctor. But that was not why I came. My name is Lucan. I am writing a book, and I was hoping you could help me."

"A book?" She said without surprise. "Then you had better come in."

Lucan picked up his luggage: his doctors' bag, his knapsack, and a smaller leather roll, which accidentally unravelled and spilled a number of paint-brushes, paint-pots, rolls of papyrus and writing implements.

"My book," he said apologetically, gathering up the mess.

"I see you are also a painter," said the lady, stooping gracefully to help him.

She led him into a simple parlour and offered him a chair. It was late December and although there was a watery sunlight it was cold. She started to work up a fire.

"I imagine you want to know about my son," she said. "Many books have been written about him, but you are the first writer who has come to ask me. There are many things I could tell you. Perhaps you will stay a few days?"

"I should be honoured, but I do not want to be a burden. You seem to live alone here."

"Yes and no. I have a great many nephews and nieces who help me, and of course my son's friends visit often. They have promised that they will all be here with me when my time runs out."

"I have already spoken to some of them. I came here with my friend Paul, but he is now in prison. I visit him regularly to treat him, but he seems all right for a few days, and so I have been visiting others. Peter sends his fondest regards. I have been trying to find out as much as possible from those who were there from the beginning, but nobody was as much at the beginning as you."

"That is not quite true," she said with a laugh. "Methuselah was also there at the beginning."

"Methuselah?"

She motioned him through a door. "This is the way," she said. A corridor led into a small back room. It was dark because the shutters were closed. Pushing them open, she pointed to a grassy courtyard, in the middle of which was an ancient ox, who immediately heaved himself up, ambled over to the window, and stuck his grizzled head in through it.

"Methuselah," she said, stroking his muzzle affectionately. "He was a present from the innkeeper when my son was born. We have kept him ever since. My son used to ride on his back. I keep the shutters closed because he always sticks his head in to find out what's going on."

"This will be your room," she continued. She pointed at a flat table by the window. "You can use that to write on - careful Methuselah doesn't munch your papyrus. My husband and son made it together," she added proudly. "The top lifts off and the legs dismantle."

Lucan sat on the bed, and the old lady sat down on the only chair in the room. He took out a scrap of papyrus.

"I heard that even kings came to see you when your son was born?"

"No. There were certainly no kings. A great many came with presents, mostly local shepherds. But there were others too, who had travelled great distances, probably because of the Census. Some of them, I daresay, were very wise, well-to-do people. But no kings. I sat in the stable, with my little one in my arm, just like this."

She crooked her left arm, and pointed with her right hand to the imaginary baby.

"I knew then that this little boy was the way to the future, and so did all who came. The angels praised God that night. It is a coincidence you are here today. Tomorrow would have been his birthday."

The doctor had been making notes, but struck by the beauty and poise of the old lady, he instead started sketching her. As he did so, he went on asking her questions. What was he like as a boy? What about the miracles? He knew some of the stories - were they all true? Were there others he had not heard of? What about his friends? Absorbed in his drawing, he did not note everything down, and later found he had forgotten some of it.

Before long it was quite dark, and the old lady suggested some supper before bed. The doctor declined.

"But I have one more favour to ask," he said. "Have you anything like a board I could paint on?"

She thought for a moment. "Of course, you can have the top of the desk, which detaches."

"Oh no, I could not use such a precious thing."

"You are going to make it more beautiful with a picture, not less."

She bade him good night and left the room. Lucan sat at the desk, finishing his notes, with Methuselah the Ox still peering in through the window. When he had finished, he detached the desk top and, propping up his sketches, began to paint.

He painted Mary as he could see she must have been that morning, more than fifty years before, with the little boy in her left hand, her right pointing at him, as if to say, as she indeed had said to him "This is the way". He painted all night and was finishing when, next morning, Mary knocked at his door.

"Madam," he said, "If I had been there that morning, this is what I would have given your baby. Please accept it now on His birthday."

**Zacchaeus in the Sycomore Awaiting the Passage of Jesus
by James Tissot, circa 1890**

2. THE TAX COLLECTOR

It is a hot, thirteen-mile, sometimes uphill journey from Jerusalem to Jericho, but you can do it by noon if you start early along the Roman road with its frequent springs and cisterns. When Lucan reached the point where the valley opens out and he could see the city walls, he tried to imagine them tumbling at a trumpets' blast. It was pleasant to pass through the gate into the elegant streets beyond, shady with sycamore trees laden with figs. An agreeable scent of balsam wafted out of some of the shops. Large numbers of priests sauntered about among the crowds of shoppers.

He found the tavern he was looking for and asked the innkeeper for Zacheus. He pointed to an elderly little man who was sitting at a table outside eating olives.

"I know who you must be, Doctor," he said glancing at Lucan's medicine-bag. "My friend Matthew Levi told me all about you. You're another scribbler like him. Have some lunch?" said the old man, pointing at a chair. They talked pleasantries while lunch was brought out. Behind the humorous twinkle in his eyes, there was perhaps something melancholy about him. "Do you regret giving up your job?" asked Lucan.

"You think I should? You see that large building at the end of the street?" Lucan followed his gaze towards a massive building, which might once have been a watermill but was now a small mansion. "I used to live there. And now my wife Veronica and I rent a small room upstairs here. That is the consequence of climbing trees when you are old enough to know better.... At dinner in my house, the Subject of your book told a story, about a businessman who left his money in the hands of his servants. While he was away, they didn't manage his funds and instead shopped him to the authorities. I knew exactly what He meant because I had seen people of that kind over the years in my work. But it was only then, as He spoke, that I saw that I myself was just like them. No, I don't regret leaving my job."

Many of the passers-by crossed the road when they saw them sitting there. Lucan apologised. "No, no, it's not you. They

19

wouldn't come near me anyway, even though I gave up working for the government more than fifteen years ago. Too many dealings with gentiles like you," said Zacheus cheerfully. "I used to revel in their hostility, until I met Him. He told another very good story about a man who was beaten up by robbers on the very road you have just come along; the only passer-by who bothered to stop was a Samaritan. Do you know, there are 10,000 priests living in this city, and He could have lodged with any of them. But where do you think He came to stay? There, with me!" he said pointing at the mansion again. "When they asked him why, He said 'Nobody calls a doctor if they aren't sick.'"

"I am afraid that's not quite true," said Lucan with a laugh. "If only it were."

As they ate, Zacheus told his story. How when Jesus had passed along the High Street where they were sitting, the crowds had turned out; how he had climbed one of the sycamore trees - "That very one!"- outside his house in order to catch a glimpse.

But there was something missing from his account.

"Tell me, what made you so determined to see Him? How did you know who He was?" asked Lucan. The old man hesitated.

"Well, I had seen Him once before, a very long time ago. And..." he bent over to Lucan, his voice dropping "I had something terrible on my conscience. I will tell you, but please do not mention it in your book."

The doctor nodded and looked sympathetically at the old man as he struggled for words.

"When I was young, I lived further south. All I wanted was to get as much money as I could, as soon as possible, so I got work as a debt collector and book-keeper for the local Publican. This was when Quirinius was Governor of Syria. The Romans had not been long in charge, when a decree went out from Caesar Augustus that all the world should be registered. I was appointed Registrar and set up an office in a tavern in Bethlehem, with a comfortable room for myself next door. Huge numbers of people came from all over the territory, anyone who was of David's clan. All the lodgings were completely full otherwise. A poor old man came to the inn with his lovely young bride, heavily pregnant. He tried to get a room because she was about to give birth – I overheard them pleading with the innkeeper and I could have lent them one of my rooms. But I was too selfish, and the innkeeper gave them space in a stable instead. The woman had her baby almost immediately – I went to see; she had wrapped him in swaddling clothes and laid him in a manger. It was a very strange night, very hot for the time of year. Everyone noticed a spectacular shooting-star. It was impossible to sleep for the noise of people milling about. Then a large caravan of foreigners rode in. Three of them, very wealthy-looking merchants, came to the inn and took great interest in the couple with the baby. Then they came upstairs to my rooms and demanded to see my Register. I thought it was a cheek and told them I wasn't going to open it until the following morning. I asked them their names.

""I will tell you my name, and that of my friends," said the imposing Ethiopian. "But if you want your life to be worth living, you will not write in your register either our names or the names of the family lodged in the stable, and you will not breathe a word about any of us. We are Gaspar, Melchior and I, Balthasar."

"So the following day, though they had moved off with their caravan heading, so it was said, for Egypt, I did as I had been told – I wrote down the names of every man, woman and child in the little town, except for this one family, who had also disappeared. Perhaps they had gone with the caravan.

"A few days later the Royal Guard clattered in and the Captain came straight to my lodgings. He wanted the Register too. Although it was my duty to keep it for the Romans, not for King Herod, I was afraid and handed it over. I knew something terrible was going to happen.

"Then the Captain simply looked down the list, noted every child under two, and had them butchered in the village square. I saw it with my own eyes. I told myself over and over again that it wasn't my fault, but the mothers wailed at me that I had done Herod's dirty work. How they wept; what could I do to comfort them for their lost little ones? I moved north beyond the Jordan for shame, and there I put all my energy into making money and trying to pretend the whole thing had never happened. I became a Chief Publican – one of few Jews ever to do so, and was generally hated. People said I could not call myself a Son of Abraham. And the more they despised me, the more I wanted to be despised. But all along I remembered the couple in the stable, hoping that perhaps by saving that one baby boy I had redeemed something of myself.

"When He grew up, He mixed a great deal with people in my line of work, and I got to hear about Him – my friends were of course quite well informed. In fact, at first I wondered if He was that prophet, John. So I went to see him and asked what I should do. "Stop cheating," John told me. I decided it couldn't be Him, and carried on as before.

"But then I heard that there really was a connection between John and the baby I had seen – they were second cousins. So when it was said He was passing through Jericho, I swore I would offer Him the lodging which I had failed to provide at the inn at Bethlehem. I did not really think I was worthy to receive Him, but when as He passed He saw me clinging to the sycomore, He seemed to know me already. I did not have to ask Him – He invited Himself to stay. You could hear people grumbling. I had not planned to offer Him more than dinner and a bed for the night, but the moment He spoke to me I felt I would do anything – anything at all to make amends. I shouted so that everyone could hear: "Behold, Lord, the half of my goods I give to the poor, and if I have wronged any man of anything, I restore him fourfold!" And then He said the thing I shall never forget. "This day is salvation come to this house, because he also is a son of Abraham. For the Son of Man is come to seek and to save that which was lost."

**Adoration of the Shepherds
by Lebrun, 1689**

3. THE SHEPHERDS

"Thou, Bethlehem Ephrata, art a little one among the *thousands of Juda*" said the Greek grimly, as he paused under the meagre shelter of a tall, crumbling, dry-stone tower and peered through the blinding torrent of rain, at what might just be a light from a hearth about a mile off. It was dark and he was lost. On the boat from Caesarea to Joppa he had been told that it was possible to walk along the road from Emmaus, and then across country to Bethlehem, without going along the highway to Jerusalem. But there were no signposts, the path was sometimes invisible, and every village, if such they could be called, looked the same. "No matter," he thought, as he walked through the mud of the single street. "Wherever this is, I shall have to stop here for the night." He banged on the door of the first house until an old woman opened. She looked frightened.

"Fear not," he said, as reassuringly as he could. At this the woman looked even more startled.

"An angel..." she murmured, "he said you were coming for him!" Now it was Lucan who was startled.

"Who?"

"My husband Gibea." The woman drew him in and shut the door, and then pointed to an old man lying beside a feeble fire. He was muttering in a fever.

"I am no angel, madam, but I am a doctor," said Lucan, unrolling his oilskin haversack and setting out some small boxes and pots of medicaments.

It was a cold, draughty place, only half a building, propped up against the side of a hill. Outside, some sheep bleated – he could catch the occasional glint of their eyes, reflected in the firelight as they peered through the cracks in the dilapidated wattle wall. They were evidently penned in a cave in the hill, which opened out next to the house. Soaked as he was, Lucan paid no further attention to his surroundings until he had done what he could to help the old shepherd. He gave him willow leaves and urged him to chew. The old man did so intermittently, still mumbling. Lucan then sat down on the only bench in the room, and the old woman brought him dry clothes, bread, salt, and a pot of beer.

"*Sikera*," he said with a smile.

"You speak our language?" Asked the woman, in good but antiquated Greek.

"No, but I am a ship's doctor, and the word for beer is the first thing one learns in any port."

"We are a long way from the sea. What brought you here?"

"Our prayers have brought him here! A man of good will!" shouted the recumbent figure by the fire with sudden energy, before subsiding back into unconsciousness. Luke turned back to the woman.

"I have been writing a book about the man they call Jesus Christ. I never met him myself, so I started to read what accounts I could get hold of. But not all of them seem reliable, so it seemed a good idea to try to talk to people who had actually known him, and had seen all things from the beginning. I spoke to his mother, and she said he was born in Bethlehem. Is this the village? Do you know anything about it?"

"Not in this village," said the old woman, "in this very house, or, to be exact, in the cave over there where we pen the sheep." She pointed at the wattle partition where the bleating came from. Lucan could not disguise his surprise.
"I see this was not what you were expecting the birthplace of the Prince of Peace to look like. Don't worry, I take no offence. In my father's day this was the finest tavern in a fine little town – the City of David! I could almost say it was magnificent, a caravanserai with stables for stallions, mares and camels, and quarters fit for an Imperial legate or an eastern princeling on a mission to Egypt."

"What became of it, if you don't mind me asking?" said Lucan.

"One year, when I was sixteen, a decree arrived from Caesar Augustus, that all those of the House of David should be enrolled for taxation. So we spent weeks making preparations to receive extra guests. We turned the stables into guestrooms, and the cave by the house into a stable, but as the time approached the town filled up and there was no room left at the inn.

"One Joseph came up from Galilee, out of the city of Nazareth, all the way here to Judaea, because he was of the house and family of David, to be enrolled with Mary, his fiancée, who was with child. And it came to pass, as they got here, her days were accomplished, that she should be delivered. At first my father turned them away, but Joseph pleaded with such force that at length he said he would make up a bed for them in the stables. There was no time to lose. She brought forth her firstborn son and wrapped him in swaddling clothes, and laid him in a manger."

"I heard that even Kings came to worship him?"

"We had some very grand visitors, some from a great way off, and quite a few came to peep at the child and brought gifts. Even the ox and the ass poked their heads over the partition – my father presented the couple with the ox. I gave them a basket of eggs. But I was not interested in the rich strangers, I had eyes only for one of the shepherds who came down from the country, where they had been keeping the night watches over their flock." As she said this, she looked fondly at the comatose old man. "Perhaps you saw the Migdal Eger as you walked over the valley?"

"I sheltered for a while under an old stone tower up there. Was that it?" The woman nodded.

"Rachel's Pillar. That was where my husband's family kept the flock which was used for the Temple sacrifices. He has told me so often what happened then. He and his brothers were standing on top of the tower, watching a great shooting star, when behold! An angel of the Lord stood by them, and the brightness of God shone round about them; and they feared with a great fear. And the angel said to them 'Fear not!'"

"So that is why you mistook me for an angel, " said Lucan.

"Well, yes," answered the old woman simply, "he said an angel would come tonight, and that I should not be afraid. He's dying, isn't he?"

"We shall see. Perhaps the fever will break. We can only wait." Talking seemed to quieten her, so he coaxed her to continue.

"The Angel told them: 'This day is born to you a Saviour, who is Christ the Lord, in the city of David. And this shall be a sign unto you. You shall find the infant wrapped in swaddling clothes, and laid in a manger.' So of course, the shepherds said one to another 'Let us go over to Bethlehem, and let us see this word that is come to pass, which the Lord hath shewed us.' And they came with haste, and found Mary and Joseph, and the infant lying in the manger. That was how I met my husband. He burst in carrying a lamb as a gift for the baby, and told us everything, and we all wondered at the child and what the shepherds had said. They did not stay long, because they had to return to the flock. But as they walked back, glorifying and praising God for all the things they had heard and seen, I knew then in my heart that Gibea was for me. But it was a long time before I could see him again. Soon after the couple left with their baby, soldiers arrived and there was a terrible massacre. They ransacked the inn, and left it half burned down. My father died of grief soon afterwards. For a long time I could feel nothing but bitterness for this 'Prince of Peace.'"

"I heard about this terrible event," said Lucan. He wanted to change the subject. "What happened to the angel after he delivered his message?"

"My husband always said that suddenly a multitude of the heavenly host appeared, praising God and saying..." At this point she was interrupted by a loud shout from the old man by the fireplace,

"Glory to God in the highest! And on earth peace to men of good will! Can you see them?"

The old woman ran over to her husband and cradled his head in her lap. "What can you see, Gib my darling?" Lucan looked round at the creaking walls, the dripping ceiling and the lambs' eyes glinting through the wattle. There was nothing to see, but suddenly he felt strangely warmed in this freezing place.

"He's dead," said the woman with a sob. And so it seemed, but Lucan put his wrist on the old man's forehead and then felt his pulse.

"No, the fever has broken. He is fast asleep. Get some rest, I'll look after him." The old woman walked unsteadily to the door of the only other room in the house. Before going in she turned, her eyes streaming with tears. "I haven't slept for three days. If you are not an angel, surely you were sent by one, for my husband is right. You are truly a man of good will. Peace be to you."

Journey of the Magi
By James Tissot, 1894

4. THE MAGI

i. John

Lucan wanted to stay longer with John in his cave overlooking the haven at Patmos, but he was the Ship's Doctor on this voyage and the tide was on the ebb. The sailors were already bustling to weigh anchor, their shouts just audible on the mild breeze.

"I have to go. I'm sorry to have been here only these few minutes."

"Send me a copy of your book when it is finished. There are so many things which He did; which, if they were written every one, the world itself, I think, would not be able to contain the books that should be written. If I remember anything of importance which you have left out, I'll be sure to leave a note of it."

"Just one thing before I go," said Lucan. "I have sometimes heard that wise men or kings came from the east to worship at the crib. Do you know anything about this?"

John stared silently into the blue for so long that Lucan wondered if he had heard. At length he said,

"Find Thomas; he has been travelling in the East."

ii. Thomas

When Lucan found Thomas, it was not as he expected. He was in a sorry state, sitting in the market of a small Palestinian village wearing barely more than a turban, eating a mushroom and talking nonsense. A crowd of small boys was running around him poking fun. The more he talked, the more they sniggered.

"Yes!" he cried angrily, "He walked through the wall, as if there were no wall at all! He wasn't really there you see, just a spirit. It looked like Him, but you couldn't touch Him because He wasn't there." The small boys fell about laughing. Lucan strode over and brushed them away like so many flies. Thomas lifted his yellowish, bloodshot eyes.

"Do you believe what you are telling them?" asked the doctor.

"I don't believe anything I can't touch. The only thing I have is this."

Reaching into his bosom Thomas pulled out a grimy papyrus with a kind of almanack drawn on it. Lucan recognised it as the priest-rota from the Book of Paralipomenon. Five places were marked, the feasts of Passover, Pentecost and Atonement; and the two weeks when the Abia priest-clan served.

"I see the Three Great Feasts are specially marked; but why the two courses of Abia?"

"That was how they forecast the date of Jesus' birth."

"Who?"

"King Gaspar and the other Magi." Thomas' eyes dilated again and he seemed to be thinking of something else.

"Please, tell me how you got this," urged Lucan.

"The others all believed what they saw. Jesus soaring up to the sky crying 'Go ye unto all the world!' I had no idea what to think. So I decided not to think, but to do, and I made for the farthest corner of the earth. I took service as a carpenter with Habban the architect who was building a palace for King Caspar Gundophorus at Taxila on the Indus.

"When the King heard I had known Jesus before His death, he summoned me. He was very old. He sat on a divan, like a cat with glittering eyes. I was afraid, but to my surprise he said he had been a follower of Jesus too. I told him that in that case he needed no palace, for he already had a house of many mansions. It was this remark which prompted him to tell me his story, and this is what he said."

iii. Caspar Gundophorus

In the 3755ᵗʰ Year of Creation, by the Hebrew reckoning, I, Caspar of the Five Rivers, then Chief of the Magi of Tarshish, called my brothers-in-priesthood Balthasar of Sheba and Melchior the Persian, as was our custom, to cast a horoscope for the future and the coming King of Kings. Two questions only concerned us: when would he be born, and where?

"He shall be called a Nazarene" said I

"A Virgin shall bring forth child," added Balthasar.

"Aye, but first," quoth Melchior, "comes Elijah the prophet, the Forerunner."

This seemed to mean we should seek not one, but two births. I shall not say by what black arts we proceeded, for I am now ashamed of them and their consequences. But we divined that the first child would be born to a Priest of the Course of Abia, conceived after he had served in the Temple of Jerusalem, and the second six months later. Since each Priestly Clan served a course on its own twice a year, and thrice yearly all the four-and-twenty Clans served a course together, there were five possible days in the year for the birth of the Forerunner. How should we decide which was the right day? It was Balthasar who solved this difficulty.

"Let us consider the purpose of the first child's coming," he said. "Malachias continues, 'He shall turn the heart of the fathers to the children, and the heart of the children to the fathers'. Is this not the work of the Day of Atonement? That is the 10th day of Tishri; but the boy could not be conceived until the feast of Tabernacles on 21st. Tishri, or 25ᵗʰ September by the Roman calendar. But in which year?"

We had no answer. But as we gazed out of my palace window into the night sky, Melchior said

"Is that not the King of Heaven's Star? When will it proceed out of Virgo?" So we ransacked all the books of the Chaldees and found that somewhere over to the west, near Jerusalem, Jupiter, the "King of Heaven" would be at his meridian in the mid-point of Virgo, 15 months after the Day of Atonement of that very year, during Quirinius' governorship of Syria. Surely that would mark the birth of the second child, the Christ-King of Heaven, six months after his Forerunner. But where would the meridian be?

"We shall have to go to that country and find it," I said.

Our preparations took so long that we had no time to look for the first child, the Forerunner. I heard he grew up practically orphaned in the desert. We made straight for where we hoped to find the baby king himself. Never was such a caravan seen! For the divine child, Balthasar had a hundredweight of frankincense brought by ship, with milk-white camels to bear it; the mournful Melchior had great chests full of Myrrh, slung across the silk and leather saddles of a train of his finest horses. And I took all the gold from my palace, a gift for a new emperor, as I imagined him. It was months before we set out, travelling westwards, across the Jordan, then south to Jerusalem, where we came to the court of King Herod.

"Where is he that is born king of the Jews?" demanded Balthasar in a voice of thunder, "for we have seen his star in the east, and are come to adore him."

Hearing this, King Herod, and his courtiers, seemed troubled. He dismissed us and called together all the chief priests and scribes and inquired where Christ should be born. At length they gave him an answer:

"In Bethlehem of Juda. For so it is written by the prophet: 'And thou Bethlehem in the land of Juda art not the least among the princes of Juda: for out of thee shall come forth the captain that shall rule my people Israel.'"

Then Herod called us back for a private audience. Balthasar had courage, but not cunning, and was about to reveal our predictions, so I interrupted.

"Tell us first, your majesty, what you know of the place, and we will tell you of the time."

The king looked at me sharply, and then said

"Bethlehem."

But I decided not to be so straight. If only I had had the honesty of Balthasar! I said only that we had seen the star during the past two years. This seemed to satisfy the King.

"Go and diligently inquire after the child, and when you have found him, bring me word again, that I also may come to adore Him," he said.

So we went our way; and each midnight we looked up to see where the Star of the King of Heaven stood. When we came to Bethlehem, we looked down the village well outside the local inn, and behold, there in the reflection of the water we saw the Star, right in the centre of the constellation of the Virgin. And we rejoiced with exceeding great joy. And entering into the house, we found the child with Mary His mother, and falling down we adored Him; and opening our treasures, offered Him the gifts; gold, frankincense, and myrrh. But that night I slept badly; over and over again I saw Herod's sly, inquiring sneer, and in the morning I said to my brother-priests

"That man worships no-one. We will tell him nothing. Let us not return to Herod, but return another way." After we left, so we were told, an angel appeared in a dream to Joseph, saying

"Arise, and take the child and His mother, and fly into Egypt, for Herod will seek the child to destroy him."

But when Herod perceived that we had deluded him, he was exceedingly angry; and sent his guards to kill all the men children that were in Bethlehem, and in all the countryside around, from two years old and under, according to the time which I had told him. If I had only been more exact, the slaughter would have been less; and if we had kept our promise to return, there would have been no bloodshed at all, because the Holy Family had already escaped, though not through any advice from us. So now you see why I don't dabble in horoscopes, and I always tell the whole truth: for it is not for me to look into the mind of God.

*   *   *

"I cannot tell the whole story," said Lucan.

"Why, don't you want to tell the whole truth? Or do you doubt it?" asked Thomas anxiously.

"As John said to me recently, there is no room to write down everything, and I have already promised someone not to write about the bloodshed. You will have to ask someone else to do that."

**The Tree of Jesse Contemplated by the Prioress
of the Haarlem Magdelenes
by Jan Mostaert, 1485**

5. THE FAMILY TREE

"What *have* you done?" said Paul looking up at his Doctor as he stepped in from the crowded Roman alleyway into his cluttered lodging. The Doctor pulled up a chair and sat down. Paul was twitching nervously and looked as if he were on the verge of a fit.

"You should not be working," said Lucan soothingly to his patient, who was sitting at a table covered in tablets and papers. "What's the matter? Another Stoic polemic from our friend Seneca?"

"The matter," said Paul testily, "is that your researches are causing chaos. Look, here's another letter from Timothy. He says there is the most amazing rumpus in Ephesus about your genealogical tables. Please Lucan, tell me, what have you done?"

Lucan smiled as he thought back. It was always a pleasure to recall his travels in Palestine, where he had trodden so closely in Jesus' footsteps that he could almost feel he knew him. He thought of his visit to Bethlehem, and how later he had called on Mary herself.

"While you were in prison in Caesarea, I was researching for my life of Jesus, and I came across several versions. One of them started with a genealogy of Joseph which was taken from the Tax Office. I asked what was the point of that, if Joseph wasn't His father? The tax official I spoke to, Zacchaeus, said that as Jesus was legally the son of Joseph, he was legally of David's line. When I visited His mother, I asked about this and she said that anyway, she was also of David's line. She produced the family tree of her father Eli. So I began my life of Jesus with her genealogy instead of Joseph's."

"Yes, but that is not all you did, is it?" At this, Lucan seemed to struggle with himself for an instant.

"No. I took the opportunity to complete the genealogy back as far as Adam, the father of us all, to show that we are all one flesh with Jesus, Jew and Gentile alike. Surely you, of all people, the Apostle to the Gentiles, can have no objection?"

"I have never understood why you take so much trouble over the details of Jesus' life. I don't. What is true is true, and no amount of evidence can make it truer. 'If this be of men, it will come to nought; but if it be of God, you cannot overthrow it' as Rabbi Gamaliel always used to say. Do you know what he also told me? When Pontius Pilate was lucky enough to have Jesus standing in front of him and could have asked him any question he liked, he said Stop that!"

"Stop that?" said Lucan, looking up from a scrip of paper from which he was making notes. "No, Lucan, stop taking notes! He said 'What is truth?' Believe me, you will never convince anyone with your story."

"It's very easy for people who have met Jesus to say that. But those who knew Him are dying like flies, and people like me who never met Him want a record that we can trust."

"Why? I have never met Him either, at least, not in any way that would satisfy your readers. If you want truth of the kind which purges the soul and wipes away the past," said Paul, pausing before adopting a lofty tone, "you must not give heed to fables and endless genealogies, which furnish questions rather than the edification of God, which is in faith. There," he said, grabbing a stylus, "I am going to write to Ephesus to tell them so. Perhaps that will stop them claiming what they call special knowledge!" Paul was beside himself.

"Calm down, my friend," said Lucan, "Write whatever you like, I am sure it will be appreciated by all those Ephesian intellectuals. But do not be so hard on the rest of us who want a story, about a little town in Bethlehem where, as I have learned, an innkeeper made room for a worried couple in his stable and where angels brought the very same tidings you are sending in your letters, not to Ephesus, but to shepherds."

The Presentation in the Temple
by Ludovico Carracci, 1605

6. NUNC DIMITTIS

A crowd, mostly of pilgrims, was standing on the broad stone
stairway next to the building which housed the Pool of Siloam; it
was hot, and Lucan wondered if it was worth waiting for a turn
to wash. But he pressed on up, towards the looming Temple
whose southern wall beat back the rays of the noonday sun.
There was a break in the steps, but the street still led uphill, until
presently he came to the ceremonial staircase leading up to the
Double Gate. Just off the staircase, to the right, was a shady open
structure, built of cedars supporting a canvas awning. Scribes
and students were seated about, people came and went. It was
busy and in the middle of it all was a jolly old man, hopping
about, now talking encouragingly to one of his pupils, now
talking to a stranger who looked in. At the same time he was
dictating at least two different letters to two scribes who sat
patiently waiting for each phrase or sentence as it came.
Lucan tapped one of the onlookers on the shoulder.

"Is that Rabbi Gamaliel?"

"Certainly," the man answered, "and when he passes away, so
will purity and piety."

 For a moment Lucan watched the old man dictating.

"Johanan, write to the Galileans: 'It is high time we had in the
olive tithes. You are holding up the sacrifice; we have reduced
the price of turtledoves for women after childbirth, but the tithes
are due in fair measure.'" He turned to Lucan. "Fair measure: I
always give people three pieces of advice: get yourself a teacher,
rid yourself of doubt, and don't fool yourself about the fair
measure of a tithe. Does that help you?" he asked jovially.

"I did not come for advice, though I heard you also usually tell
people not to bother with Scripture unless they have learned a
proper trade."

"True my friend, but I see you are a doctor, so you do not need to
learn anything from me on that score."

43

"Certainly I have found that theology is useless if you cannot apply it to life; and life is toil."

"Ah, a Mediterranean Fish! A Gentile, who has read and understood! But if you did not come for advice, why did you come?"

"First of all, I bring greetings from a former pupil of yours, my friend and patient Saul, or Paul as he now calls himself. "

"I remember him! He was an ideological young man. I told him 'theories get people killed. Go and learn a trade – try being a tentmaker, and see if work teaches you something which I cannot.'"

"He took your advice, and sends you his fondest regards."

"Good, good, and where is he now?"

"In prison," said Lucan, with a smile. "He was arrested in connection with his preaching; he is now a follower of Jesus of Galilee, as am I. In fact, this was the other matter that brought me to you. I know you were very kindly disposed towards my fellow-religionists, and I wanted to ask why. I am planning a book."

"You are speaking, I suppose, of the trial of Peter before the Sanhedrin? Well, perhaps I have a soft spot for your sect. But I have always believed that God does not need us to defend him. These are troubled times, and if people go on pointing the accusing finger, there will be bloodshed. I once saw your Jesus make exactly this point, just down the road. I was walking on my way to work when I saw him talking outside the Pool of Siloam. Pontius Pilate had just executed some Galileans for treason, and someone was claiming this proved they were enemies of God. Jesus pointed at the ruins of the tower which had fallen down a few days before, which had also killed some Galileans. He said 'These things happen; they prove nothing about God.' I was very impressed."

"And that is the only reason why you urged the Sanhedrin to let Peter and his friends off and leave God to deal with them?"

The Rabbi looked at him sharply, but after a moment his glance softened.

"My friend, if you want to know another reason, I will tell you a story about my late father, Rabbi Simeon. He was very learned; he wanted to be as great a scholar as his father, Rabbi Hillel. But he used to come home each day, saying "What is the point of it all? When I was young I had a premonition that I would see the Messiah in my own lifetime. But now I am old I see it will not happen." But he died happy, and I shall tell you why. One day, when I was about nine years old, not long before he died, he was in the Temple and a couple came in with a child to be circumcised. He took the child in his arms as if it were his own, and looked as if he would never let go. Then he laughed a great laugh, which I had never seen him do before. 'Lord, now lettest Thou Thy servant depart in peace,' he said 'for mine eyes have seen Thy salvation, which Thou hast prepared before the face of all people, to be a light to lighten the Gentiles, and to be the glory of Thy people, Israel.'"

Gamaliel spread his hands before him in a conclusive gesture.

"That was the infant Jesus, and if He is your light and our glory, who am I to stand in the Sanhedrin and criticise?"

The Visitation
by Piero di Cosimo, 1490

7. MAGNIFICAT

Sitting on the shady little terrace Mary was reminiscing. She and Lucan had been talking of John the Baptist and his parents. Her house was a solid stone building on a hill off the road which sloped away steeply. In the distance they could see Ephesus, which seemed to lie on rising ground approached by narrow paths which wound up to an uneven plateau, where the towering Temple of Diana suddenly reflected the setting Sun. The sight interrupted their conversation and they paused to watch. Lucan remembered from his schooldays a line of Antipater, and quoted half to himself: *"When I saw the house of Artemis that mounted to the clouds, those other marvels lost their brilliancy, and I said, "Lo, apart from Olympus, the Sun never looked on aught so grand."*

But somehow those stirring old sentiments seemed to have lost their thrill, now that he was here, talking face to face about things that mattered in real life. They went back to their conversation.

"I was very fond of my cousin Elizabeth," said Mary, smoothing the folds of her blue and red dress "though we were so many years apart. She lived in a house in the hill country of Juda. I thought of her on the day of my betrothal. I wondered if the same fate would befall me, to be childless past the age of childbearing, and hear the taunts of the neighbours."

She got up and, reaching up to a shelf, pulled out an old scroll which she held up.

"I took out this old copy of the Book of Samuel and in the second chapter I was reading the Song of Hannah," she said unrolling the scroll and looking for a passage. Finding it she continued: *"They that were full before have hired out themselves for bread; and the hungry are filled, so that the barren hath borne many; and she that had many children is weakened."*
" 'Perhaps,' I thought to myself, 'no word shall be impossible with God.'" She looked up from the scroll and fixed her dark eye on Lucan.

"Suddenly, Gabriel walked in. He was wearing one of those togas that retired legionaries often wear. As in a dream I knew who he was without being told, and he said 'Hail, full of grace, the Lord is with thee; blessed art thou among women.' His voice was kindly but the gravity of his demeanour frightened me. Also, I had been thinking of poor Elizabeth. Yes, how blessed I was compared to her, on the threshold of a new life, full of hope. Gabriel saw my confusion and said 'Fear not'..."

"Angels always say that," interrupted Lucan.

She nodded. "He told me that I was conceiving a boy, what to call him, and said that he would ascend the throne of David and reign forever," she said, her matter-of-factness out of keeping with the vastness of the statement.

"What did you think of that, what did you say?" asked Lucan.

"I said 'How shall this be done, because I know not man?'"

A fair question, thought Lucan. Aloud he said "Did you find yourself with child..." he grasped for the delicate word "... immediately?"

She seemed to ignore the question but went on "The angel said 'The Holy Ghost shall come upon thee, and the power of the most High shall overshadow thee. And therefore also the Holy which shall be born of thee shall be called the Son of God.' I wasn't really comprehending, but then he said something which was the sweetest thing I could wish for."

"And what was that?" asked Lucan, wondering what this extraordinary woman could have thought would be sweeter than the news the angel had already brought her.

"He said, 'Behold thy cousin Elizabeth, she also hath conceived a son in her old age, because no word shall be impossible with God.' I lost no time getting ready to visit her, to bring her the news. I could not help thinking how like Hannah she was, and on the journey over to Juda I made up a song for her. Of course, when I got to her house she made a great fuss over me and made out that my news was even more marvellous than hers. So I sang her my song."

Then in a clear, strong and unembarrassed voice the old lady opened her mouth and sang. Lucan thought he had never heard such a lovely hymn. It seemed to weave together all the strands of Mary's strong personality; she sang of the mighty, the holy and the merciful; the admiration of generations, the humbling of the proud and the exaltation of the humble. A song for her friend and cousin; a song for anyone. He told her so.

"I often wonder where the words of a song come from. They certainly don't seem to come from inside, so I don't think anyone can claim to own a song," she replied. "Pass it on to Peter and the others if you think they would like it."

"Thank you, I will. And we shall be sure to sing it on the mornings when we remember your Son's nativity, if not, indeed, daily." She looked pleased but suddenly very tired. For a moment a window had been opened to Lucan, but he felt that for now he could not ask for more than that.

"I am writing it down, I hope you don't mind," he said, scratching at one of his wax tablets as he did so:

My soul doth magnify the Lord, and my spirit hath rejoiced in God my saviour...

EXPLANATORY NOTES

1. MARY

1. *I am a doctor*
St Luke was, according to St. Paul's letter to the Colossians (4:14), a doctor, and from the Second Letter to Timothy (4:11) it is clear that St. Paul was his patient.

2. *My name is Lucan*
The probable name of the Third Evangelist was Lucanus (English Lucan), for which Luke (Greek Loukas) was a nickname.

3. *I see you are also a painter*
The tradition that St. Luke was a painter is very ancient. In the 4th century, the Empress Eudoxia possessed a portrait of the Virgin Mary reputedly painted by him on an old table-top, of which several copies survive. They show the Virgin pointing to her Son, and are known as Hodegetria "pointers to the way." St. Luke is, naturally, the patron saint of painters and doctors.

4. *Many books have been written about him*
So St. Luke himself says in the opening words of his Gospel

5. *they will all be here with me*
There is an ancient tradition that the Twelve Apostles reassembled at her bedside, at the time of her Dormition or Assumption.

6. *I have already spoken to some of them*
From details recorded by St. Luke and no-one else (e.g. Luke 22:61), it is practically certain that he had at least interviewed St. Peter.

7. *but he is now in prison*
This story is set just after St. Paul's arrest in Jerusalem under the Governor Claudias Lysias in AD 58

8. *I have been trying to find out as much as possible from those who were there from the beginning*
As he noted in his Gospel (1:2)

9. *an ancient ox*
The traditional symbol of St. Luke. Also, thanks to Isaiah's statement "The ox knoweth his owner, and the ass his master's crib" (Isaiah 1:3), these two animals are usually shown in scenes of the Nativity.

2. THE TAX COLLECTOR

1. The basis of this story is to be found in Luke, 19:1-10.
2. *along the Roman road with its frequent springs and cisterns*
I have never been to the Holy land but I understand these facts to be correct according to the latest archaeology.
3. *he tried to imagine them tumbling at a trumpets' blast.*
Joshua 6:20
4. *shady with sycomore*
Luke's original Greek says Sycomore, a type of fig tree, not the more common Sycamore.
5. *An agreeable scent of balsam*
Archaeologists confirm that Balsam was the principal commodity traded in Jericho in the First Century
6. *Large numbers of priests*
Archaeology confirms this: about 10,000 members of the priestly caste resided in Jericho at this time (see later in the story).
7. *an elderly little man*
Luke 19:3 "he was low of stature"
8. *My friend Matthew Levi*
According to Luke 5:27, the apostle identified in Matthew's Gospel as Matthew himself was a tax-gatherer surnamed Levi, one of the priestly clan. The story of Zacchaeus, however, is told only by Luke, and not referred to in Matthew's Gospel.
9. *a watermill*
My little joke: I have been renovating a watermill for years. The building in Jericho traditionally owned by Zacchaeus is still to be seen, and is an impressive house at the end of the main street.
0. *my wife Veronica*
According to (probably mediaeval) tradition, Veronica, who had wiped the sweat of Jesus' brow on the road to Calvary, later married Zacchaeus.
1. *the Subject of your book told a story*
Luke 19:11 *et seq.*
2. *a Samaritan*
The story of the Good Samaritan is only recorded by Luke, not the other evangelists (Luke 10:30 *et seq.*)
3. *Nobody calls a doctor if they aren't sick*
Luke 5:31
4. *please do not mention it in your book*
Luke omits both the Magi and the Massacre of the Innocents from his account; these elements of the story are only to be found in Matthew's gospel.
5. *when Quirinius was Governor of Syria*
Luke, writing in Greek, calls him Kyrenios. See also note 19 to chapter 4.
6. *a decree went out from Caesar Augustus*
This statement of Luke's (2:1) is commonly thought to refer to the Census, which was conducted primarily to make taxation easier.
7. *We are Gaspar, Melchior and I, Balthasar.*
These are the traditional names of the Magi. The Gnostic Gospel of Thomas mentions a King Gundophorus, a historical character, properly called

Gundophernes but elsewhere known as Gasparus or Casparus, as a soothsaying King who converted to Christianity.

8. How they wept.
Matthew 2:18 "A voice in Rama was heard, lamentation and great mourning; Rachel bewailing her children, and would not be comforted."

19. He mixed a great deal with people in my line of work
Luke (15:1-2) records that "the publicans and sinners drew near unto him to hear him. And the Pharisees and the scribes murmured, saying: This man receiveth sinners, and eateth with them."

20. "Stop cheating," John told me.
Luke 3:13

21. they were second cousins
Luke 1:36

22. I did not really think I was worthy to receive Him
An allusion to Luke 7:6, which is thrice repeated at Mass, with beaten breast, just before the moment of Communion: *"domine non sum dignus..."*

3. THE SHEPHERDS

1. Thou, Bethlehem Ephrata, art a little one among the thousands of Juda
Micah 5:2. The prophet continues: "out of thee shall he come forth unto me
that is to be the ruler in Israel: and his going forth is from the beginning, from
the days of eternity."
2. Without going along the highway from Jerusalem.
i.e. without taking the path between Jerusalem and Emmaus along which Luke
would later record that Jesus first revealed Himself after the resurrection, to
Cleopas and a disciple that Luke does not name.
3. a tall, crumbling, dry-stone tower
This building, the Migdal Eder ("flock-tower"), is still to be seen and
traditionally marks the grave of Rachel. Jacob watered his flocks nearby. It was
used by shepherds to watch their flocks by night. From this part of the country
came the lambs used in the Temple sacrifices in Jerusalem.
4. the boat from Caesarea to Joppa
This story is set at the time when Paul, who was Luke's patient, was imprisoned
at Caesarea (AD 58-60), having been transferred there from Jerusalem.
5. Fear not
The traditional greeting of angels, addressed by them to Hagar, to Zacharias
when he was in the Temple, to Mary at the Annunciation, to the Shepherds at
the Nativity, also heard by Abraham, and by Moses before the Burning Bush.
6. My husband Gibea
Gibea was Caleb's grandson and consequently a well-known name in the area
around Bethlehem of which he was the patriarch. In the mediaeval Wakefield
Mystery Plays, Gib is the name given to one of the shepherds in the Second
Shepherd's play. This is presumably a lucky coincidence.
7. penned in a cave
The traditional birthplace of Jesus, now inside the Church of the Nativity in
Bethlehem, is a cave.
8. He gave him willow leaves
The medical school of Asclepius at Tarsus, where Luke had conceivably been
trained, used willow leaves to treat fever.
9. Sikera
This is the only Aramaic word which Luke uses in his Gospel and Acts.
10. I am a ship's doctor
A plausible guess from the knowledge his writings betray of nautical terms.
*1. to talk to people who had actually known him, and had seen all things
from the beginning*
So Luke tells Theophilus in the opening paragraph of his Gospel.
2. A decree... no room left at the inn
This closely follows Luke's account. (Luke 2:1-7)
3. I heard that even Kings came to worship him?
Luke does not mention the Magi in his Gospel; they are found only in
Matthew's version.
14. You are truly a man of good will. Peace be to you.
According to Luke, the Angels proclaimed "peace to men of good will," not (as
Anglican liturgy has it) "goodwill towards men" nor (as the Vatican II Mass had
it until recently) "peace to his people on Earth."

4. THE MAGI

1. with John in his cave overlooking the haven at Patmos
St. John, "the Eagle of Patmos", was the youngest of the apostles, and by tradition the author of the Gospel according to John, the Epistles of John and the Revelation of the Apocalypse. He spent much of his later life in a cave below the hilltop temple of Diana on the island of Patmos, from which he had his vision; his account of it mentions the island.

2. the world itself, I think, would not be able to contain the books that should be written
A direct quotation from the end of John's gospel, also according to tradition written in the same cave.

3. I'll be sure to leave a note of it.
Very little of John's gospel is incorporated in the other three gospels, though Luke's gospel has more in common with John's than do the others. Both tradition and most modern scholars regard John's Gospel as the latest of the four; according to Eusebius he wrote it in order fill in the gaps left by the other three Evangelists.

4. Find Thomas; he has been travelling in the East
According to the apocryphal *Acts of Thomas*, the Apostles agreed among themselves who should preach where, and it was Thomas's lot to travel to the East. Eastern Christian communities of great antiquity assert that they were founded by him, and at Mar Thoma in Malabar on the eastern coast of India his supposed tomb has been a place of pilgrimage since at least the time of Alfred the Great, who sent an embassy there.

5. He wasn't really there you see, just a spirit
Docetism, a Gnostic heresy which claimed that Christ only seemed to be human, but was in fact a spirit, claimed to be informed by the teachings of St. Thomas. The apocryphal *Gospel of Thomas*, a forgery which may nonetheless preserve some genuine ancient stories and sayings of Jesus, fancifully describes him walking through walls. Whatever doubts or difficulties he may have had, Thomas must have resolved them to the satisfaction of the Church, for though he is known as "Doubting Thomas" he is venerated as one of the most important of her saints.

6. I don't believe anything I can't touch
According to St. John (20:24-29), Thomas doubted whether the resurrected Jesus was real, and insisted on putting his hands into the wounds in order to check.

7. the priest-rota from the Book of Paralipomenon
Paralipomenon=Chronicles. The rota can be found in 1 Chronicles 24:1-31

8. but why the two courses of Abia?"
See Luke's account of John the Baptist's birth (Luke Chapter 1). All the priests of the Temple belonged to the Tribe of Levi, which was divided into "courses", each of which took turns to serve in the Temple twice a year. John the Baptist's elderly father was serving in the Course of Abia when he was told his wife would conceive. Under ritual laws of matrimonial abstinence, the conception could not have taken place until immediately after the course was finished.

9. Go ye unto all the world!
This is the so-called Great Commission, which Mark and Matthew report but, (strangely considering his interest in world evangelism) Luke leaves out.

10. building a palace for King Caspar Gundophorus at Taxila on the Indus
According to the apocryphal *Gospel of Thomas*. It was assumed until the 1950s that Gaspar or Caspar Gundophorus was a legendary character, until excavations on the Indus unearthed coins minted in his reign at about this time.

11. a house of many mansions
John 14:2.

12. the 3755th Year of Creation, by the Hebrew reckoning
The dating and astronomical references which follow are genuine. 3755 = 6 BC, widely agreed to be two years before the year of Jesus' birth in BC 4. The traditional year of AD 1, first calculated by Dionysius Exiguus in the 6th century, is certainly wrong. It is clear from Luke's account that Jesus was born exactly six months after his cousin John the Baptist (to this day the feasts of Christmas and St. John are six months apart); therefore the first Christmas fell 15 months after the conception of John the Baptist.

13. He shall be called a Nazarene
Matthew 2:23 says that it was prophesied that the Messiah would be called a Nazarene, but the source of this prophecy is now lost.

14. A Virgin shall bring forth child
Isaiah 7:14

15. "first," quoth Melchior, "comes Elijah the prophet, the Forerunner
This prophecy of Malachias (Malachi) 4:5 was, according to Matthew, fulfilled by John the Baptist (Matthew 11:14)

17. 10th day of Tishri
The Hebrew calendar varies from year to year, but in the year 6 BC, the 21st day of the month of Tishri fell on 25th September.

18. the "King of Heaven" would be at his meridian in the mid-point of Virgo
The coincidence that at Bethlehem on December 25th, Jupiter, "the King of Heaven" proceeded out of the constellation of Virgo, at an angle of 68 degrees to the horizon, was first noticed by Kepler in 1606. The year of this conjunction is however disputed.

19. Quirinius' governorship of Syria
Publius Sulpicius Quirinius was Consul in BC 12. His subsequent career is not wholly known. He was Legate in Syria, possibly not for the first time, from AD 6-12 and died in AD 21.

20. practically orphaned in the desert
Luke says "the child grew, and was strengthened in spirit; and was in the deserts until the day of his manifestation to Israel." (1:80)

21. Where is he that is born king of the Jews? Et seq
The source for this passage is the second chapter of Matthew's Gospel

22. thou Bethlehem in the land of Juda art not the least...
Matthew 2:5-6; he was quoting Micheas (Micah), 5:2

23. When we came to Bethlehem, we looked down the village well
King David's Well at Bethlehem stands beside the supposed burial place of King David, and marks the spot where, according to 2 Samuel 23, David's army broke through a Philistine garrison to fetch water. The well was rediscovered in 1895.

24. You will have to ask someone else to do that
Luke does not record the Massacre of the Innocents, which is only mentioned by Matthew.

5. THE FAMILY TREE

1. said Paul looking up at his Doctor
We know from Colossians 4:14 that Luke treated Paul when he was in Rome awaiting trial. This story is set in the optimistic interlude when Paul was temporarily released from house arrest, around A.D. 61.

2. as if he were on the verge of a fit
It is not recorded what illness St. Paul suffered from. He called it his "thorn in the flesh" (2 Corinthians 12:7) and it made him the object of derision. Some have suggested epilepsy.

3. Seneca
The Stoic writer Seneca was educated, like Paul, at the university of Tarsus where they were both almost certainly pupils of Athenodorus of Tarsus. This accounts for similarities in some of their writings. A correspondence between Paul and Seneca exists, but is probably a fourth century forgery.

4. Timothy
Timothy, possibly a kinsman of Luke, was in charge of the Church at Ephesus.

5. the most amazing rumpus in Ephesus
There is some debate as to what heresy had beset the Ephesians, but they made much of genealogies. They may have been interested in the Gnostic idea that Jesus was the last of a series of emanations from God; or they may have been Judaizers, attempting to restrict Christianity only to those of Jewish descent.

6. He thought of his visit to Bethlehem...
There is no record of Luke having travelled in Palestine or visited Mary but the fact that he did may be inferred from his writings.

7. While you were in prison in Caesarea
Paul was imprisoned in Caesarea, where he appeared before the Procurator Felix, from AD 58-60. It is a plausible speculation that Luke used this period to research for his Gospel, in between medical visits to his patient.

8. I began my life of Jesus with her genealogy instead of Joseph's
The differences between the Genealogies of Jesus contained in the respective Gospels of Matthew and Luke have been explained by the fact that Matthew (a tax collector) used a legal document concerned with Joseph's family, while Luke used a genealogy of Mary. On this theory, Joseph's father was Jacob, a descendent of David through King Solomon, and Joseph's father-in-law, i.e. Mary's father, was Heli, also a descendent of David but through Solomon's brother Nathan. This is a feasible interpretation because, as Joseph was an old man, his father would have been dead at the time of Jesus' birth; but in Jewish law he would have been the heir and therefore the son "in law" of Mary's father, if the latter had no other children (which, so far as we know, he had not).

9. the Apostle to the Gentiles
Paul was appointed Apostle to the Gentiles at Antioch in AD 48. He was sensitive to the criticism that having never known Jesus in his earthly life, he could not really call himself an Apostle.

0. I have never understood why you take so much trouble over the details of Jesus' life. I don't.
Apart from Jesus' Last Supper, death and resurrection, Paul never refers to any event of Jesus' life in any of his copious writings.

1. 'If this be of men, it will come to nought; but if it be of God, you cannot overthrow it'

By his own statement (Acts 22:3), Paul was a pupil of the famous Rabbi Gamaliel, whose remark, reported by Luke and quoted here, was made in the Sanhedrin, when he urged the Jewish authorities not to persecute Peter and the other Christians (Acts 5:38-39).

2. What is truth?

This saying of Pilate's is recorded by John (18:38). Its rhetorical character reveals the speaker as a relativist.

3. people like me who never met him

Luke admits in his preface that he never met Jesus, but only people who knew him.

4. I have never met him either, at least, not in any way that would satisfy your readers

According to Luke (Acts 9:3-18 and elsewhere, since the story is repeated) Paul met Jesus in a vision on the road to Damascus. In his first letter to the Corinthians (I Corinthians 15:8) Paul insists that this was a real meeting.

5. you must not give heed to fables and endless genealogies

This line was indeed written by Paul to Timothy at Ephesus (1 Timothy 1:4)

6. Write whatever you like

It has sometimes been speculated, on the basis of stylistic similarities, that Luke helped Paul write some of his letters.

7. but to shepherds

The Lucan account of the nativity. Matthew, by contrast introduces the Magi.

8. PICTURE: The Tree of Jesse

Trees of Jesse, or "Jesses", are the origin of the Christian use of the Christmas Tree, sometimes still called a Jesse Tree. At the root, where modern custom would place the crib, lies the sleeping Jesse, father of King David. On the branches are some or all of the 43 generations which Luke records between Jesse and Mary, including Solomon with his peacock, symbolising wisdom. At the top, where nowadays we would place an angel or star, is Mary with the Infant Jesus. The sight of the confusing panoply of characters probably gave rise to the derisory song *The Twelve Days of Christmas*.

6. NUNC DIMITTIS

1. *Pool of Siloam*
The Pool of Siloam was a reservoir fed from the Spring of Gihon via a covered channel, constructed by King Hezekiah in about 700 BC as Sennacherib was about to lay siege to Jerusalem. According to St. John's Gospel, Jesus healed a beggar and then sent him to wash in its waters, which suggests that the Pool was used as a ritual bath (*Mikvah*). He may also have been prophesying the Roman destruction of Jerusalem by alluding to Isaiah 8:6: *Forasmuch as this people hath cast away the waters of Siloe, that go with silence....therefore behold the Lord will bring upon them the waters of the river strong and many, the king of the Assyrians, and all his glory: and he shall come up over all his channels, and shall overflow all his banks* (etc). It was a convenient source of fresh water, open to the public, on the way up to the Temple. It was excavated in 2004.

2. *the ceremonial staircase leading up to the Double Gate*
Remains of the Double Gate are still visible on the south side of the Temple Mount, approached by a broad staircase leading up from the Pool of Siloam.

3. *Johanan, write to the Galileans*
Johanan ben Nuri was a scribe under Gamaliel and was so learned that it was thought he could estimate the number of drops of water in the sea. It is said that if you dream of him, you can be sure to develop an aversion to sin. This note of Gamaliel to the Galileans is recorded in the collection of Jewish oral traditions known as the Mishnah.

4. *get yourself a teacher, rid yourself of doubt, and don't fool yourself about the fair measure of a tithe*
This saying of Rabbi Gamaliel's is recorded in the Mishnah.

5. *a Mediterranean Fish! A Gentile, who has read and understood*
According to the Mishnah, Rabbi Gamaliel compared his pupils to four classes of fish:
- A ritually impure fish: one who has memorised everything by study, but has no understanding, and is the son of poor parents
- A ritually pure fish: one who has learnt and understood everything, and is the son of rich parents
- A fish from the Jordan River: one who has learnt everything, but doesn't know how to respond
- A Mediterranean fish: one who has learnt everything, and knows how to respond

6. *I have a soft spot for your sect*
According to tradition, he was later baptised as a Christian and is regarded by the Catholic Church as a Saint. This tradition is supported by the fact that he is not held by Jews to have passed on the chain of oral Jewish tradition to which he was a prominent heir.

7. *if people go on pointing the accusing finger, there will be bloodshed*
As He climbed the hill to His own execution, Jesus warned the women following Him of exactly this, prophesying the destruction of Jerusalem: "Daughters of Jerusalem, weep not over me; but weep for yourselves, and for your children." (Luke 23:28). The Romans razed the city some 35 years later.

8. *God does not need us to defend him*
See Note 11 to the previous story.

9. *the tower which had fallen down a few days before, which had also killed some Galileans*
Luke recorded this story, not mentioned by other writers, in his book (Luke 13:4)

10. *my late father, Rabbi Simeon*
Gamaliel's father was indeed called Simeon and an ancient tradition asserts that this was the same Simeon who, according to a story which only Luke records, first sang the *Nunc Dimittis* as described here.

1. *his father, Rabbi Hillel*
Gamaliel was the Grandson of Rabbi Hillel whose dictum "That which is hateful to you, do not do to your fellow. That is the whole Torah; the rest is the explanation" was, so Luke records, quoted by Jesus (Luke 6:31)

60

7. MAGNIFICAT

1. They could see Ephesus
Ancient tradition holds that Mary spent her last years living near Ephesus, cared for by St. John the Evangelist. The 19th century mystic Anne Catherine Emmerich, better known for her vision of the Passion which Mel Gibson followed in his film, had a vision of the house. Archaeologists found it as described, though Emmerich had never been near the place.

2. The towering Temple of Diana
The original Temple of Diana (or Artemis) at Ephesus was one of the Wonders of the World, but was burnt down by a megalomaniac who wanted to be remembered for doing so. In Luke's time its successor was still spectacular and served a particular cult of Artemis of the Ephesians. Luke reports (Acts 20) that St Paul caused a riot there among silversmiths who were losing their trade in miniature shrines as a result of the spread of Christianity. The spiritual void left by the demise of the Cult of Diana has been filled by that of the Virgin Mary. *3. My cousin Elizabeth*
According to Luke's Gospel (1:36), John's mother Elizabeth was Mary's cousin. There was thus a blood kinship as well as a theological kinship between Jesus and John.

4. The hill country of Juda
So Luke informs us (Luke 1:39)

5. The Song of Hannah
It has long been noticed that the *Magnificat* or "Song of Mary" owes much to the *Song of Hannah* recorded in the First Book of Samuel, 2:1-10. By tradition, Mary is always portrayed as reading a book at the time of the Annunciation.

6. One of those togas that retired legionaries wear
I imagined this detail owing to the remarkable circumstance that two friends of mine, unknown to each other, have had visions of a messenger in a de-mob suit.

7. Hail, full of grace, the Lord is with thee; blessed art thou among women
This greeting, recorded by Luke (1:28), is the origin of the *Ave Maria*

8 "Fear not"
See note 4 to Chapter 3.

9. I sang her my song
The *Magnificat* is recorded by Luke alone (Luke 1:46-55)

10. We shall be sure to sing it on the mornings
In the Western Church the *Magnificat* forms part of the daily morning office.

www.ingramcontent.com/pod-product-compliance
Lightning Source LLC
Chambersburg PA
CBHW041025170626
46815CB00001B/8